FLICKA, RICKA, DICKA

AND THE STRAWBERRIES

FLICKA, RICKA, DICKA
AND THE STRAWBERRIES

BY MAJ LINDMAN

ALBERT WHITMAN & COMPANY
CHICAGO, ILLINOIS

Flicka, Ricka, and Dicka were three little girls who lived in Sweden long ago. They had blue eyes and golden curls, and they always dressed alike.

One day, they played in the garden all morning. Then they came in to ask if they might go on a picnic.

Mother stood in the sunny kitchen with empty jars before her. There were big jars and little jars, and they were all empty.

"I am wondering what fruit I can find to fill all of these jars," Mother said.

"I know—wild strawberries!" said Flicka. "We'll pick them for you."

Mother stood in the sunny kitchen with empty jars before her.

Long after they were in bed, they were still talking.

"We want to go on a picnic anyway," said Ricka. "It will be more fun to pick strawberries at the same time. We'll go early tomorrow."

"We will each pick a big basketful," promised Dicka.

Mother smiled. "That will be very nice," she said. "And I will pay you for each basket." Then she promised to pack a picnic lunch.

The three little girls ran to find their baskets. They talked all afternoon about where they would go to find the largest strawberries. Long after they were in bed, they were still talking.

Right after breakfast, Flicka, Ricka, and Dicka started on their way to pick wild strawberries.

Each little girl carried her own basket. Flicka carried the picnic lunch in a brown leather bag.

"It will be so much fun to have our own money," said Flicka.

"There are lots of things that we could buy," said Ricka.

Dicka was the last to leave. She fastened the garden gate and waved good-bye to Mother.

She fastened the garden gate and waved good-bye.

There were flowers in the woods, and the birds sang. But the three little girls did not find many wild strawberries.

"We will never get these big baskets filled here," said Flicka.

"We must go to the pasture on the hill," said Ricka.

They hurried to the pasture. There on the sunny hillside, ripe wild strawberries grew everywhere. Each little girl began to fill a basket.

Ripe wild strawberries grew everywhere.

The three little girls ate their picnic lunch among the bluebells.

They picked wild strawberries all morning. They ran from one sunny spot to another, and they always found more big, red berries.

"My basket is heavy!" said Flicka.

"Mine is nearly full," said Ricka.

"I don't think I can carry any more," said Dicka. "And I am hungry."

"Let's have our picnic lunch here under this tree," said Flicka.

The three little girls ate their picnic lunch among the bluebells. They had slices of bread with meat and cheese, and sweet milk to drink.

Flicka, who had been ahead, came running back.

It was late afternoon when they walked along a twisting path toward home. They had gone much farther than they thought. It began to grow dark among the trees.

Ricka sat down on a stone. Big tears rolled down her cheeks as she cried, "I am hot and tired! I want to be home."

"I know! We have walked miles. I am very tired, too," said Dicka. "Perhaps this wasn't the right path for us to take."

Then Flicka, who had been ahead, came running back. "Come quickly," she called. "Just over the hill is a little cottage. We can get a drink, and someone there can surely tell us how to go home."

A little girl and a much smaller little boy came out.

Ricka stopped sobbing. The three little girls started walking down the path toward the cottage.

When they came to the front steps, Flicka called, "Will someone please help us?"

The door opened. A little girl and a much smaller boy came out.

"What can we do for you?" the girl asked.

"We are very tired and thirsty," said Ricka. "May we have a drink of cold water, please?"

"And I'm afraid we've also gotten lost," continued Dicka. "Could you show us the shortest path through the woods?"

"Come in, please," the girl said. "Mother will be glad to help you."

Flicka, Ricka, and Dicka went into the cottage. A smiling woman came and poured them each a cup of water. Her apron was very clean and neatly patched.

The dress the little girl was wearing was patched in many places, too.

"I wish I could give you milk, but I don't always have enough for the baby," said the woman. "Mary, my little girl, will be glad to take you through the woods. It's not that far."

The three little girls thanked her. Then they followed Mary through the woods. Soon they could see the garden gate and their home. They all thanked Mary and said, "We'll see you soon."

A smiling woman poured them each a cup of water.

The three little girls helped her.

Mother was very glad her three little girls were back. She said, "I have never seen such fine, big berries, nor such full baskets!"

The next morning, she cooked all the berries in a big kettle. She filled every jar, and the three little girls helped her. As they worked, they told her all about Mary and her family.

When the wild strawberries were all in jars, Mother gave each little girl a silver coin. "You have earned this," she said. "It is yours to spend as you like."

Then Flicka, Ricka, and Dicka began to talk about what they wanted most. They talked all through the day. And they talked long after they had gone to bed.

As Mother was getting into bed, the three little girls rushed in to see her.

"We don't really need anything at all, Mother," said Flicka. "We have toys and dresses and plenty to eat."

"But Mary needs a new dress," said Ricka, "and the little boy has no toys."

"May we spend our money for them?" asked Dicka softly.

Mother smiled. "Of course! The money is yours. I am glad you are so generous. Now run to bed; tomorrow we'll go shopping."

The three little girls rushed in to see her.

The next morning, Mother took Flicka, Ricka, and Dicka to the dress shop. They chose a red dress with a white collar and cuffs.

"I know Mary will like the bright red belt and the big dots," said Flicka.

Then they bought a soft brown bear at the toy shop. "That's just right for the baby," said Ricka.

At home, Mother filled a basket with oranges, milk, cookies, and a jar of fresh strawberry jam!

They chose a red dress with a white collar and cuffs.

Flicka, Ricka, and Dicka gave out all the presents.

That afternoon, the three little girls went through the woods to Mary's cottage. Flicka carried the basket. Ricka carried the new dress all tied up in a big box. Dicka carried the toy bear.

Mary met them at the door. In a moment, they were all inside the cottage, and Flicka, Ricka, and Dicka gave out all the presents.

Mary eagerly held up her dress. The baby sat rocking the brown bear.

"Such wonderful gifts!" said Mary's mother. "You girls and your mother must come over and share this strawberry jam."

"We will!" said Dicka. Then Flicka, Ricka, and Dicka, and their new friend, Mary, ran out to the woods to play.

Then Flicka, Ricka, and Dicka, and their new friend, Mary, ran out to play.

The FLICKA, RICKA, DICKA BOOKS
By MAJ LINDMAN

FLICKA, RICKA, DICKA AND THEIR NEW SKATES
FLICKA, RICKA, DICKA AND THE STRAWBERRIES
FLICKA, RICKA, DICKA AND THEIR NEW FRIEND
FLICKA, RICKA, DICKA AND THE BIG RED HEN
FLICKA, RICKA, DICKA AND THE NEW DOTTED DRESSES
FLICKA, RICKA, DICKA AND THE THREE KITTENS
FLICKA, RICKA, DICKA AND THE LITTLE DOG
FLICKA, RICKA, DICKA BAKE A CAKE
FLICKA, RICKA, DICKA GO TO MARKET

Library of Congress Cataloging-in-Publication Data
Lindman, Maj.
Flicka, Ricka, Dicka and the strawberries / Maj Lindman.
p. cm.
Summary: Three little girls go off on a picnic to pick
wild strawberries, and with the money they earn buy
gifts for a poor family they met in the woods.
ISBN 0-8075-2499-9
[1. Helpfulness—Fiction. 2. Sisters—Fiction.
3. Triplets—Fiction. 4. Sweden—Fiction.] I. Title.
PZ7.L659 Flh 1996 [E]—dc22
96002705
Hardcover edition: 978-0-8075-2512-8
Based on original design by Stephanie Bart-Horvath

For more information about Albert Whitman & Company,
visit our web site at www.albertwhitman.com.